MOTHER GOOSE

NURSERY RHYMES

FALL RIVER PRESS

New York

An Imprint of Sterling Publishing
387 Park Avenue South
New York, NY 10016

ISBN: 978-1-4549-0980-4

Printed and bound in China.

1 3 5 7 9 10 8 6 4 2

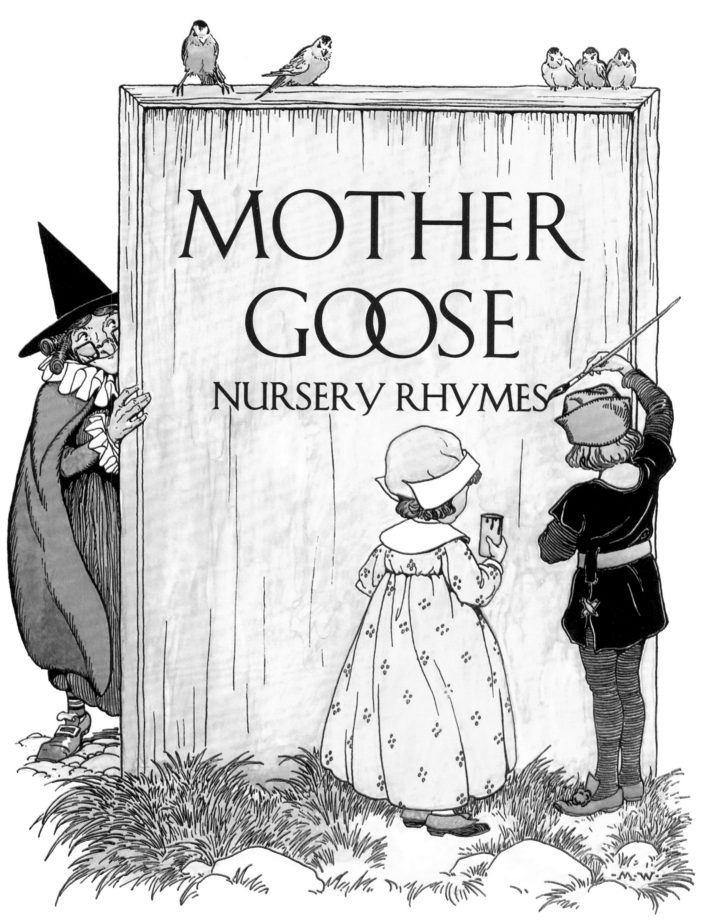

MOTHER GOOSE
NURSERY RHYMES

Illustrated by Blanche Fisher Wright

FALL RIVER PRESS

New York

CONTENTS

LITTLE BO-PEEP 1
LITTLE BOY BLUE 1
SEE-SAW 1
THE CLOCK 2
WINTER 2
FINGERS AND TOES 2
A SEASONABLE SONG 2
DAME TROT AND HER CAT 3
THREE CHILDREN ON THE ICE 3
CROSS PATCH 3
THE OLD WOMAN UNDER A HILL 3
TWEEDLEDUM AND TWEEDLEDEE 3
OH, DEAR! 4
OLD MOTHER GOOSE 4
LITTLE JUMPING JOAN 4
PAT-A-CAKE 4
MONEY AND THE MARE 4
ROBIN REDBREAST 4
A MELANCHOLY SONG 6
JACK 6
GOING TO ST. IVES 6
THIRTY DAYS HATH SEPTEMBER 7
BABY DOLLY 7
BEES 7
COME OUT TO PLAY 7
IF WISHES WERE HORSES 9
TO MARKET 9
OLD CHAIRS TO MEND 9
ROBIN AND RICHARD 10
A MAN AND A MAID 11
HERE GOES MY LORD 11
THE CLEVER HEN 11
TWO BIRDS 13
LEG OVER LEG 13
LUCY LOCKET 13
WHEN JENNY WREN WAS YOUNG 13
BARBER 14
THE FLYING PIG 14
SOLOMON GRUNDY 14
HUSH-A-BYE 15
BURNIE BEE 15
THREE WISE MEN OF GOTHAM 15
THE HUNTER OF REIGATE 15
LITTLE POLLY FLINDERS 16
RIDE AWAY, RIDE AWAY 16
PIPPEN HILL 16
PUSSY-CAT AND QUEEN 16
THE WINDS 16
CLAP HANDIES 18
CHRISTMAS 18

ELIZABETH 18
JUST LIKE ME 18
PLAY DAYS 18
HEIGH-HO, THE CARRION CROW 19
A B C 20
A NEEDLE AND THREAD 20
BANBURY CROSS 20
THE MAN IN OUR TOWN 20
GEORGY PORGY 22
FOR EVERY EVIL 22
CUSHY COW 22
WEE WILLIE WINKIE 23
ABOUT THE BUSH 23
SIMPLE SIMON 25
THREE BLIND MICE 25
FIVE TOES 25
A LITTLE MAN 26
DOCTOR FOSTER 26
DIDDLE DIDDLE DUMPLING 27
JERRY HALL 27
LENGTHENING DAYS 27
THE BLACK HEN 29
THE MIST 29
A CANDLE 29
MISS MUFFET 29
CURLY-LOCKS 29
HUMPTY DUMPTY 30
ONE, TWO, THREE 31
THE DOVE AND THE WREN 31
MASTER I HAVE 31
PINS 31
SHALL WE GO A-SHEARING? 31
GOOSEY, GOOSEY, GANDER 33
OLD MOTHER HUBBARD 33
THE COCK AND THE HEN 34
BLUE BELL BOY 34
WHY MAY NOT I LOVE JOHNNY? 35
JACK JELF 35
JACK SPRAT 37
HUSH-A-BYE 37
DAFFODILS 37
THE GIRL IN THE LANE 37
HUSH-A-BYE 37
NANCY DAWSON 38
HARRY THE GREAT 39
THE ALPHABET 39
DANCE TO YOUR DADDIE 40
ONE MISTY MOISTY MORNING 40
ROBIN HOOD AND LITTLE JOHN 40
RAIN 40

THE OLD WOMAN FROM FRANCE 42
TEETH AND GUMS 42
THE ROBINS 42
THE OLD MAN 42
T'OTHER LITTLE TUNE 43
MY KITTEN 43
IF ALL THE SEAS WERE ONE SEA 43
PANCAKE DAY 45
A PLUM PUDDING 45
FOREHEAD, EYES, CHEEKS, NOSE,
    MOUTH, AND CHIN 45
TWO PIGEONS 45
A SURE TEST 46
LOCK AND KEY 46
THE LION AND THE UNICORN 46
THE MERCHANTS OF LONDON 46
I HAD A LITTLE HUSBAND 47
TO BABYLON 47
I'LL TELL YOU A STORY 47
A STRANGE OLD WOMAN 47
SLEEP, BABY, SLEEP 48
CRY, BABY 48
BAA, BAA, BLACK SHEEP 48
LITTLE FRED 48
THE CAT AND THE FIDDLE 50
DOCTOR FELL 50
A COUNTING-OUT RHYME 50
JACK AND HIS FIDDLE 51
BUTTONS 51
HOT BOILED BEANS 51
LITTLE PUSSY 52
SING A SONG OF SIXPENCE 52
TOMMY TITTLEMOUSE 54
THE DERBY RAM 54
THE HOBBY-HORSE 55
THE MULBERRY BUSH 55
YOUNG LAMBS TO SELL 55
BOY AND THE SPARROW 56
OLD WOMAN, OLD WOMAN 56
THE FIRST OF MAY 56
SULKY SUE 58
THE HOUSE THAT JACK BUILT 58
SATURDAY, SUNDAY 59
LITTLE JENNY WREN 61
THE OLD WOMAN AND THE PEDLAR . . 61
BOBBY SNOOKS 62
THE LITTLE MOPPET 62
I SAW A SHIP A-SAILING 63
A WALNUT 63
THE MAN IN THE MOON 63

One, He Loves....................63
Bat, Bat........................63
Hark! Hark!.....................65
The Hart........................65
My Love.........................65
The Man of Bombay...............65
Poor Old Robinson Crusoe!.......66
A Sieve.........................66
My Maid Mary....................66
A Difficult Rhyme...............66
Pretty John Watts...............67
Good Advice.....................67
I Love Sixpence.................67
Bye, Baby Bunting...............67
Tom, Tom, the Piper's Son.......67
Comical Folk....................68
Cock-Crow.......................68
Tommy Snooks....................68
The Three Sons..................70
The Blacksmith..................70
Two Gray Kits...................70
One, Two, Buckle My Shoe........70
Cock-a-Doodle-Do!...............71
Pairs or Pears..................71
Belleisle.......................71
Old King Cole...................73
See, See........................73
Dapple-Gray.....................73
A Well..........................73
Coffee and Tea..................73
Pussy-Cat Mew...................73
The Little Girl with a Curl.....74
Dreams..........................74
A Cock and Bull Story...........74
For Baby........................74
Myself..........................75
Over the Water..................75
Candle-Saving...................75
Fears and Tears.................77
The Kilkenny Cats...............77
Old Grimes......................77
A Week of Birthdays.............77
A Chimney.......................77
Ladybird........................77
The Man Who Had Naught..........78
The Tailors and the Snail.......78
Around the Green Gravel.........78
Intery, Mintery.................78
Caesar's Song...................78
As I Was Going Along............79
Hector Protector................79
Billy, Billy....................79
Rock-a-Bye, Baby................79
The Man in the Wilderness.......79

Little Jack Horner..............80
The Bird Scarer.................80
Mary, Mary, Quite Contrary......80
Bessy Bell and Mary Gray........80
Needles and Pins................82
Pussy-Cat and the Dumplings.....82
Dance, Thumbkin, Dance..........82
Mary's Canary...................83
The Little Bird.................83
Birds of a Feather..............83
The Dusty Miller................84
A Star..........................84
The Greedy Man..................84
The Ten O'Clock Scholar.........84
Cock-a-Doodle Do................86
An Icicle.......................86
A Ship's Nail...................86
The Old Woman of Leeds..........87
The Boy in the Barn.............87
Sunshine........................87
Willy, Willy....................87
Tongs...........................88
Jack Jingle.....................88
The Quarrel.....................88
The Pumpkin-Eater...............88
Shoeing.........................90
Betty Blue......................90
That's All......................90
Bedtime.........................91
Dance, Little Baby..............91
My Little Maid..................91
For Want of a Nail..............91
Pease Porridge..................92
Ring a Ring o'Roses.............92
The Crooked Sixpence............92
This Is the Way.................92
Ducks and Drakes................94
The Donkey......................94
If..............................94
The Bells.......................95
Little Girl and Queen...........95
The King of France..............95
Peter Piper.....................97
One to Ten......................97
An Equal........................97
The Tarts.......................97
Come, Let's to Bed..............98
Little Maid.....................98
What Are Little Boys Made Of?...98
Bandy Legs......................99
The Girl and the Birds..........99
A Pig..........................100
Jenny Wren.....................100
Little Tom Tucker..............100

Where Are You Going,
    My Pretty Maid?............102
The Old Woman of Gloucester...102
Multiplication Is Vexation.....103
Little King Boggen.............103
Whistle........................103
Bell Horses....................103
Taffy..........................103
The Robin......................104
The Old Woman of Harrow........104
Young Roger and Dolly..........104
The Piper and His Cow..........106
The Man of Derby...............106
The Coachman...................106
There Was an Old Woman.........106
A Thorn........................107
The Old Woman of Surrey........107
The Little Mouse...............107
Boy and Girl...................108
When...........................108
Sing, Sing.....................110
London Bridge..................110
March Winds....................110
The Balloon....................111
A Cherry.......................111
The Lost Shoe..................111
Hot Codlins....................111
Miller and Mouse...............113
A..............................113
Mary's Lamb....................113
Willy Boy......................114
Polly and Sukey................114
The Death and Burial of
    Poor Cock Robin............114
The Mouse and the Clock........115
Hot-Cross Buns.................117
Bobby Shaftoe..................117
The Bunch of Blue Ribbons......117
The Woman of Exeter............118
Sneezing.......................118
Pussy-Cat by the Fire..........118
When the Snow Is on
    the Ground.................118
Robin-a-Bobbin.................119
John Smith.....................119
The Year.......................119
Handy Pandy....................121
A Nick and a Nock..............121
The Seasons....................121
Billy, Billy...................121
Rain...........................121
Jack and Jill..................121
The Farmer and the Raven.......122
Christmas......................122

SEE-SAW

MOTHER GOOSE
NURSERY RHYMES

LITTLE BO-PEEP

Little Bo-Peep has lost her sheep,
And can't tell where to find them;
Leave them alone, and they'll
    come home,
And bring their tails behind them.

Little Bo-Peep fell fast asleep,
And dreamt she heard them bleating;
But when she awoke, she found
    it a joke,
For still they all were fleeting.

Then up she took her little crook,
Determined for to find them;
She found them indeed, but it made
    her heart bleed,
For they'd left all their tails
    behind 'em!

It happened one day, as Bo-Peep
    did stray
Unto a meadow hard by—

There she espied their tails, side
    by side,
All hung on a tree to dry.

She heaved a sigh, and wiped her eye,
And over the hillocks she raced;
And tried what she could, as a
    shepherdess should,
That each tail should be properly
    placed.

LITTLE BOY BLUE

Little Boy Blue, come, blow your
    horn!
The sheep's in the meadow, the cow's
    in the corn.
Where's the little boy that looks after
    the sheep?
Under the haystack, fast asleep!

SEE-SAW

See-saw, Margery Daw,
Sold her bed and lay upon straw.

FINGERS AND TOES

Every lady in this land
Has twenty nails, upon each
    hand
Five, and twenty on hands and
    feet:
All this is true, without deceit.

A SEASONABLE SONG

Piping hot, smoking hot.
What I've got
You have not.
Hot gray pease, hot, hot, hot;
Hot gray pease, hot.

THE CLOCK

There's a neat little clock,—
In the schoolroom it stands,—
And it points to the time
With its two little hands.

And may we, like the clock,
Keep a face clean and bright,
With hands ever ready
To do what is right.

WINTER

Cold and raw the north wind
    doth blow,
Bleak in the morning early;
All the hills are covered with snow,
And winter's now come fairly.

DAME TROT AND HER CAT

Dame Trot and her cat
Led a peaceable life,
When they were not troubled
With other folks' strife.

When Dame had her dinner
Pussy would wait,
And was sure to receive
A nice piece from her plate.

THREE CHILDREN ON THE ICE

Three children sliding on the ice
Upon a summer's day,
As it fell out, they all fell in,
The rest they ran away.

Oh, had these children been at
      school,
Or sliding on dry ground,
Ten thousand pounds to one penny
They had not then been drowned.

Ye parents who have children dear,
And ye, too, who have none,
If you would keep them safe abroad
Pray keep them safe at home.

CROSS PATCH

Cross patch, draw the latch,
Sit by the fire and spin;
Take a cup and drink it up,
Then call your neighbors in.

THE OLD WOMAN UNDER A HILL

There was an old woman
Lived under a hill;
And if she's not gone,
She lives there still.

TWEEDLEDUM AND TWEEDLEDEE

Tweedledum and Tweedledee
Resolved to have a battle,
For Tweedledum said Tweedledee
Had spoiled his nice new rattle.

Just then flew by a monstrous crow,
As big as a tar barrel,
Which frightened both the
      heroes so,
They quite forgot their quarrel.

OH, DEAR!

Dear, dear! what can the matter be?
Two old women got up in an
    apple-tree;
One came down, and the other
    stayed till Saturday.

OLD MOTHER GOOSE

Old Mother Goose, when
She wanted to wander,
Would ride through the air
On a very fine gander.

LITTLE JUMPING JOAN

Here am I, little jumping Joan,
When nobody's with me
I'm always alone.

PAT-A-CAKE

Pat-a-cake, pat-a-cake,
Baker's man!
So I do, master,
As fast as I can.

Pat it, and prick it,
And mark it with T,
Put it in the oven
For Tommy and me.

MONEY AND THE MARE

"Lend me thy mare to ride a mile."
"She is lamed, leaping over a stile."

"Alack! and I must keep the fair!
I'll give thee money for thy mare."

"Oh, oh! say you so?
Money will make the mare to go!"

ROBIN REDBREAST

Little Robin Redbreast sat upon a tree,
Up went Pussy-cat, down went he,
Down came Pussy-cat, away Robin
    ran,
Says little Robin Redbreast: "Catch
    me if you can!"
Little Robin Redbreast jumped upon
    a spade,
Pussy-cat jumped after him, and
    then he was afraid.
Little Robin chirped and sang, and
    what did Pussy say?
Pussy-cat said: "Mew, mew, mew,"
    and Robin flew away.

PAT–A–CAKE

A MELANCHOLY SONG

Trip upon trenchers,
And dance upon dishes,
My mother sent me for some barm,
  some barm;
She bid me go lightly,
And come again quickly,
For fear the young men should do me
  some harm.
Yet didn't you see, yet didn't you see,
What naughty tricks they put
  upon me?

They broke my
  pitcher
And spilt the
  water,
And huffed my
  mother,
And chid her
  daughter,
And kissed my
  sister instead
  of me.

JACK

Jack be nimble, Jack be quick,
Jack jump over the candlestick.

GOING TO ST. IVES

As I was going to St. Ives
I met a man with seven wives.
Every wife had seven sacks,
Every sack had seven cats,
Every cat had seven kits.
Kits, cats, sacks, and wives,
How many were going to St. Ives?

THIRTY DAYS HATH SEPTEMBER

Thirty days hath September,
April, June, and November;
February hath twenty-eight alone,
All the rest have thirty-one,
Excepting leap-year, that's the time
When February's days are twenty-
    nine.

BABY DOLLY

Hush, baby, my dolly, I pray you
    don't cry,
And I'll give you some bread, and
    some milk by-and-by;
Or perhaps you like custard, or,
    maybe, a tart,
Then to either you're welcome, with
    all my heart.

BEES

A swarm of bees in May
Is worth a load of hay;
A swarm of bees in June
Is worth a silver spoon;
A swarm of bees in July
Is not worth a fly.

COME OUT TO PLAY

Girls and boys, come out to play,
The moon doth shine as bright
    as day;
Leave your supper, and leave your
    sleep,
And come with your playfellows into
    the street.
Come with a whoop, come with
    a call,
Come with a good will or not at all.
Up the ladder and down the wall,
A half-penny roll will serve us all.
You find milk, and I'll find flour,
And we'll have a pudding in half
    an hour.

TO MARKET, TO MARKET, TO BUY A FAT PIG

IF WISHES WERE HORSES

If wishes were horses, beggars would
    ride.
If turnips were watches, I would
    wear one by my side.
And if "ifs" and "ands"
Were pots and pans,
There'd be no work for tinkers!

TO MARKET

To market, to market, to buy a fat pig,
Home again, home again, jiggety jig.
To market, to market, to buy a
    fat hog,
Home again, home again, jiggety jog.
To market, to market, to buy a
    plum bun,
Home again, home again, market
    is done.

OLD CHAIRS TO MEND

If I'd as much money as I could
    spend,
I never would cry old chairs to mend;
Old chairs to mend, old chairs
    to mend;
I never would cry old chairs to mend.
If I'd as much money as I could tell,
I never would cry old clothes to sell;
Old clothes to sell, old clothes
    to sell;
I never would cry old clothes to sell.

ROBIN AND RICHARD

Robin and Richard were two pretty men,
They lay in bed till the clock struck ten;
Then up starts Robin and looks at the sky,
"Oh, brother Richard, the sun's very high!
You go before, with the bottle and bag,
And I will come after on little Jack Nag."

A Man and a Maid

There was a little man,
Who wooed a little maid,
And he said, "Little maid, will you
    wed, wed, wed?
I have little more to say,
So will you, yea or nay,
For least said is soonest
    mended-ded, ded, ded."

The little maid replied,
"Should I be your little bride,
Pray what must we have for to eat,
    eat, eat?
Will the flame that you're so rich in
Light a fire in the kitchen?
Or the little god of love turn the spit,
    spit, spit?"

Here Goes My Lord

Here goes my lord
A trot, a trot, a trot, a trot,
Here goes my lady
A canter, a canter, a canter, a canter!

Here goes my young master
Jockey-hitch, jockey-hitch,
    jockey-hitch, jockey-hitch!
Here goes my young miss
An amble, an amble, an amble, an
    amble!

The footman lags behind to tipple ale
    and wine,
And goes gallop, a gallop, a gallop,
    to make up his time.

The Clever Hen

I had a little hen, the prettiest ever
    seen,
She washed me the dishes and kept
    the house clean;
She went to the mill to fetch me
    some flour,
She brought it home in less than an
    hour;
She baked me my bread, she
brewed me my ale,
She sat by the fire and told many a
    fine tale.

LUCY LOCKET

TWO BIRDS

There were two birds sat on a stone,
Fa, la, la, la, lal, de;
One flew away, and then there
    was one,
Fa, la, la, la, lal, de;
The other bird flew after,
And then there was none,
Fa, la, la, la, lal, de;
And so the stone
Was left alone,
Fa, la, la, la, lal, de.

LEG OVER LEG

Leg over leg,
As the dog went to Dover;
When he came to a stile,
Jump, he went over.

LUCY LOCKET

Lucy Locket lost her pocket,
Kitty Fisher found it;
Nothing in it, nothing in it,
But the binding round it.

WHEN JENNY WREN
WAS YOUNG

'Twas once upon a time, when
    Jenny Wren was young,
So daintily she danced and so prettily
    she sung,
Robin Redbreast lost his heart, for he
    was a gallant bird.
So he doffed his hat to Jenny Wren,
    requesting to be heard.

"Oh, dearest Jenny Wren, if you will
    but be mine,
You shall feed on cherry pie and
    drink new currant wine,
I'll dress you like a goldfinch or any
    peacock gay,
So, dearest Jen, if you'll be mine, let
    us appoint the day."

Jenny blushed behind her fan and
    thus declared her mind:
"Since, dearest Bob, I love you well,
I'll take your offer kind.
Cherry pie is very nice and so is
    currant wine,
But I must wear my plain brown
    gown and never go too fine."

SOLOMON GRUNDY

Solomon Grundy,
Born on a Monday,
Christened on Tuesday,
Married on Wednesday,
Took ill on Thursday,
Worse on Friday,
Died on Saturday,
Buried on Sunday.
This is the end
Of Solomon Grundy.

BARBER

Barber, barber, shave a pig.
How many hairs will make a wig?
Four and twenty; that's enough.
Give the barber a pinch of snuff.

THE FLYING PIG

Dickory, dickory, dare,
The pig flew up in the air;
The man in brown soon brought
    him down,
Dickory,
   dickory,
     dare.

HUSH-A-BYE

Hush-a-bye, baby, on the
    tree top!
When the wind blows the cradle
    will rock;
When the bough breaks the
    cradle will fall;
Down will come baby, bough,
    cradle and all.

BURNIE BEE

Burnie bee, burnie bee,
Tell me when your wedding be?
If it be to-morrow day,
Take your wings and fly away.

THREE WISE MEN OF GOTHAM

Three wise men of Gotham
Went to sea in a bowl;
If the bowl had been stronger,
My song had been longer.

THE HUNTER OF REIGATE

A man went a-hunting at
    Reigate,
And wished to leap over a high
    gate.
Says the owner, "Go round,
With your gun and your hound,
For you never shall leap over
    my gate."

PIPPEN HILL

As I was going up
     Pippen Hill,
Pippen Hill was dirty;
There I met a
     pretty Miss,
And she dropped me a curtsy.

Little Miss, pretty Miss,
Blessings light upon you;
If I had half-a-crown a day,
I'd spend it all upon you.

LITTLE POLLY FLINDERS

Little Polly Flinders
Sat among the cinders
Warming her pretty little toes;
Her mother came and caught her,
Whipped her little daughter
For spoiling her nice new clothes.

RIDE AWAY, RIDE AWAY

Ride away, ride away,
Johnny shall ride,
And he shall have pussy-cat
Tied to one side;
And he shall have little dog
Tied to the other,
And Johnny shall ride
To see his grandmother.

PUSSY-CAT AND QUEEN

"Pussy-cat, pussy-cat,
Where have you been?"
"I've been to London
To look at the Queen."

"Pussy-cat, pussy-cat,
What did you there?"
"I frightened a little mouse
Under the chair."

THE WINDS

Mister East gave a feast;
Mister North laid the cloth;
Mister West did his best;
Mister South burnt his mouth
Eating cold potato.

PUSSY-CAT AND QUEEN

CLAP HANDIES

Clap, clap handies,
Mammie's wee, wee ain;
Clap, clap handies,
Daddie's comin' hame,
Hame till his bonny wee bit laddie;
Clap, clap handies,
My wee, wee ain.

CHRISTMAS

Christmas comes but once a year,
And when it comes it brings good
cheer.

ELIZABETH

Elizabeth, Elspeth, Betsy,
and Bess,
They all went together to seek
a bird's nest;
They found a bird's nest with five
eggs in,
They all took one, and left four in.

JUST LIKE ME

"I went up one pair of stairs."
"Just like me."

"I went up two pairs of stairs."
"Just like me."

"I went into a room."
"Just like me."

"I looked out of a window."
"Just like me."

"And there I saw a monkey."
"Just like me."

PLAY DAYS

How many days has my baby to
play?
Saturday, Sunday, Monday,
Tuesday, Wednesday, Thursday,
Friday,
Saturday, Sunday, Monday.

HEIGH-HO, THE CARRION CROW

A carrion crow sat on an oak,
Fol de riddle, lol de riddle,
    hi ding do,
Watching a tailor shape his cloak;
Sing heigh-ho, the carrion crow,
Fol de riddle, lol de riddle,
    hi ding do!

Wife, bring me my old bent bow,
Fol de riddle, lol de riddle,
    hi ding do,
That I may shoot yon carrion crow;
Sing heigh-ho, the carrion crow,
Fol de riddle, lol de riddle,
    hi ding do!

The tailor he shot, and missed
    his mark,
Fol de riddle, lol de riddle,
    hi ding do!
And shot his own sow quite
    through the heart;
Sing heigh-ho, the carrion crow,
Fol de riddle, lol de riddle,
    hi ding do!

Wife! bring brandy in a spoon,
Fol de riddle, lol de riddle,
    hi ding do!
For our old sow is in a swoon;
Sing heigh-ho, the carrion crow,
Fol de riddle, lol de riddle,
    hi ding do!

BANBURY CROSS

Ride a cock-horse to Banbury Cross,
To see an old lady upon a white
　　horse.
Rings on her fingers, and bells on
　　her toes,
She shall have music wherever she
　　goes.

THE MAN IN OUR TOWN

There was a man in our town,
And he was wondrous wise,
He jumped into a bramble bush,
And scratched out both his eyes;
But when he saw his eyes were out,
With all his might and main,
He jumped into another bush,
And scratched 'em in again.

A B C

Great A, little a,
Bouncing B!
The cat's in the cupboard,
And can't see me.

A NEEDLE AND THREAD

Old Mother Twitchett had but one
　　eye,
And a long tail which she let fly;
And every time she went through
　　a gap,
A bit of her tail she left in a trap.

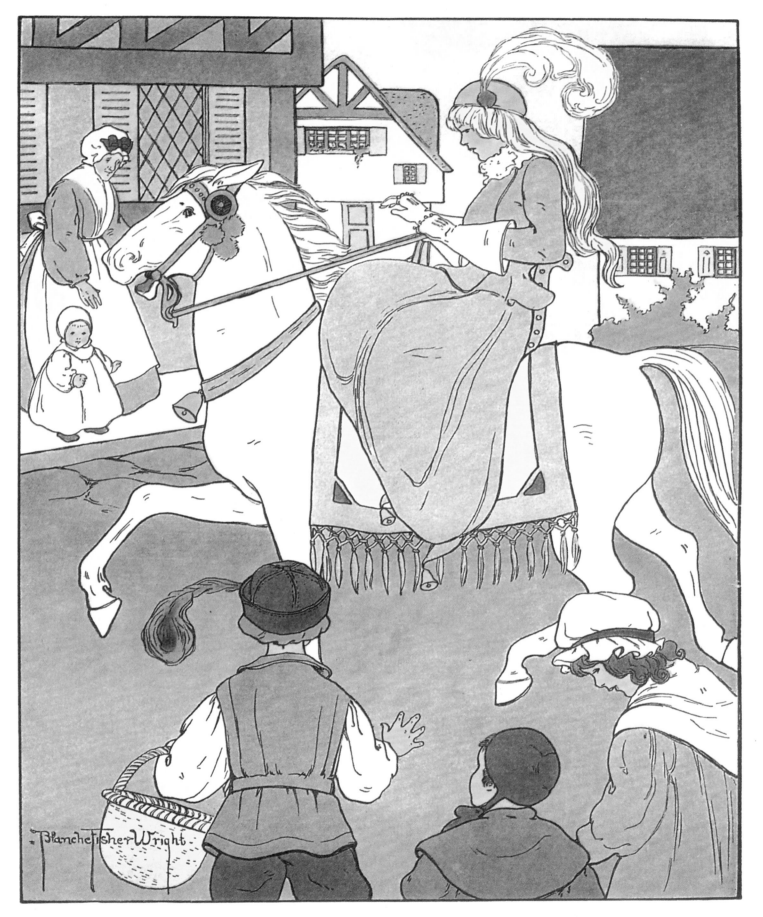

RIDE A COCK-HORSE TO BANBURY CROSS

GEORGY PORGY

Georgy Porgy, pudding and pie,
Kissed the girls and made them cry.
When the boys came out to play,
Georgy Porgy ran away.

FOR EVERY EVIL

For every evil under the sun
There is a remedy or there is none.
If there be one, seek till you find it;
If there be none, never mind it.

CUSHY COW

Cushy cow, bonny, let down thy milk,
And I will give thee a gown of silk;
A gown of silk and a silver tee,
If thou wilt let down thy milk to me.

WEE WILLIE WINKIE

Wee Willie Winkie runs
    through the town,
Upstairs and downstairs, in his
    nightgown;
Rapping at the window, crying
    through the lock,
"Are the children in their beds?
Now it's eight o'clock."

ABOUT THE BUSH

About the bush, Willie,
About the beehive,
About the bush, Willie,
I'll meet thee alive.

Then to my ten shillings
Add you but a groat,
I'll go to Newcastle,
And buy a new coat.

Five and five shillings,
Five and a crown;
Five and five shillings
Will buy a new gown.

Five and five shillings,
Five and a groat;
Five and five shillings
Will buy a new coat.

THREE BLIND MICE

SIMPLE SIMON

Simple Simon met a pieman,
Going to the fair;
Says Simple Simon to the pieman,
"Let me taste your ware."

Says the pieman to Simple Simon,
"Show me first your penny,"
Says Simple Simon to the pieman,
"Indeed, I have not any."

Simple Simon went a-fishing
For to catch a whale;
All the water he could find
Was in his mother's pail!

Simple Simon went to look
If plums grew on a thistle;
He pricked his fingers very much,
Which made poor Simon whistle.

He went to catch a dicky bird,
And thought he could not fail,
Because he had a little salt,
To put upon its tail.

He went for water with a sieve,
But soon it ran all through;
And now poor Simple Simon
Bids you all adieu.

THREE BLIND MICE

Three blind mice! See how they run!
They all ran after the farmer's wife,
Who cut off their tails with a
    carving knife.
Did you ever see such a thing in
    your life
As three blind mice?

FIVE TOES

This little pig went to market;
This little pig stayed at home;
This little pig had roast beef;
This little pig had none;
This little pig said, "Wee, wee!
I can't find my way home."

The drake was a-swimming with his
  curly tail;
The little man made it his mark,
  mark, mark.
He let off his gun, but he fired too
  soon,
And the drake flew away with a
  quack, quack, quack.

DOCTOR FOSTER

Doctor Foster went to Glo'ster,
In a shower of rain;
He stepped in a puddle, up to his
  middle,
And never went there again.

A LITTLE MAN

There was a little man, and he had
  a little gun,
And his bullets were made of lead,
  lead, lead;
He went to the brook, and saw a
  little duck,
And shot it right through the head,
  head, head.

He carried it home to his old wife
  Joan,
And bade her a fire to make, make,
  make.
To roast the little duck he had shot
  in the brook,
And he'd go and fetch the drake,
  drake, drake.

DIDDLE DIDDLE DUMPLING

Diddle diddle dumpling, my son John
Went to bed with his breeches on,
One stocking off, and one stocking on;
Diddle diddle dumpling, my son John.

JERRY HALL

Jerry Hall, he was so small,
A rat could eat him, hat and all.

LENGTHENING DAYS

As the days grow longer
The storms grow stronger.

CURLY-LOCKS, CURLY-LOCKS, WILT THOU BE MINE?

THE BLACK HEN

Hickety, pickety, my black hen,
She lays eggs for gentlemen;
Gentlemen come every day
To see what my black hen doth lay.

THE MIST

A hill full, a hole full,
Yet you cannot catch a bowl full.

A CANDLE

Little Nanny Etticoat
In a white petticoat,
And a red nose;
The longer she stands
The shorter she grows.

MISS MUFFET

Little Miss Muffet
Sat on a tuffet,
Eating of curds and whey;
There came a big spider,
And sat down beside her,
And frightened Miss Muffet away.

CURLY-LOCKS

Curly-locks, Curly-locks, wilt thou
    be mine?
Thou shalt not wash the dishes, nor
    yet feed the swine;
But sit on a cushion, and sew a fine
    seam,
And feed upon strawberries, sugar,
    and cream.

HUMPTY DUMPTY

Humpty Dumpty sat on a wall,
Humpty Dumpty had a great fall;
All the King's horses, and all the
   King's men
Cannot put Humpty Dumpty
   together again.

ONE, TWO, THREE

One, two, three, four, five,
Once I caught a fish alive.
Six, seven, eight, nine, ten,
But I let it go again.
Why did you let it go?
Because it bit my finger so.
Which finger did it bite?
The little one upon the right.

THE DOVE AND THE WREN

The dove says coo, coo, what shall
    I do?
I can scarce maintain two.
Pooh, pooh! says the wren, I've got
    ten,
And keep them all like gentlemen.

MASTER I HAVE

Master I have, and I am his man,
Gallop a dreary dun;
Master I have, and I am his man,
And I'll get a wife as fast as I can;
With a heighty gaily gamberally,
Higgledy piggledy, niggledy,
    niggledy,
Gallop a dreary dun.

PINS

See a pin and pick it up,
All the day you'll have good luck.
See a pin and let it lay,
Bad luck you'll have all the day.

SHALL WE GO A-SHEARING?

"Old woman, old woman, shall we go
    a-shearing?"
"Speak a little louder, sir, I am very
    thick of hearing."
"Old woman, old woman, shall I kiss
    you dearly?"
"Thank you, kind sir, I hear you very
    clearly."

GOOSEY, GOOSEY, GANDER

GOOSEY, GOOSEY, GANDER

Goosey, goosey, gander,
Whither dost thou wander?
Upstairs and downstairs
And in my lady's chamber.

There I met an old man
Who wouldn't say his prayers;
I took him by the left leg,
And threw him down the stairs.

OLD MOTHER HUBBARD

Old Mother Hubbard
Went to the cupboard,
To give her poor dog a bone;
But when she got there
The cupboard was bare,
And so the poor dog had none.

She went to the baker's
To buy him some bread;
When she came back
The dog was dead.

She went to the undertaker's
To buy him a coffin;
When she got back
The dog was laughing.

She took a clean dish
To get him some tripe;
When she came back
He was smoking a pipe.

She went to the alehouse
To get him some beer;
When she came back
The dog sat in a chair.

She went to the tavern
For white wine and red;
When she came back
The dog stood on his head.

She went to the hatter's
To buy him a hat;
When she came back
He was feeding the cat.

She went to the barber's
To buy him a wig;
When she came back
He was dancing a jig.

She went to the fruiterer's
To buy him some fruit;
When she came back
He was playing the flute.

She went to the tailor's
To buy him a coat;
When she came back
He was riding a goat.

She went to the cobbler's
To buy him some shoes;
When she came back
He was reading the news.

She went to the sempster's
To buy him some linen;
When she came back
The dog was a-spinning.

She went to the hosier's
To buy him some hose;
When she came back
He was dressed in his clothes.

The dame made a curtsy,
The dog made a bow;
The dame said, "Your servant,"
The dog said, "Bow-wow."

THE COCK AND THE HEN

"Cock, cock, cock, cock,
I've laid an egg,
Am I to gang ba—are-foot?"

"Hen, hen, hen, hen,
I've been up and down
To every shop in town,
And cannot find a shoe
To fit your foot,
If I'd crow my hea—art out."

BLUE BELL BOY

I had a little boy,
And called him Blue Bell;
Gave him a little work,—
He did it very well.

I bade him go upstairs
To bring me a gold pin;
In coal scuttle fell he,
Up to his little chin.

He went to the garden
To pick a little sage;
He tumbled on his nose,
And fell into a rage.

He went to the cellar
To draw a little beer;
And quickly did return
To say there was none there.

JACK JELF

Little Jack Jelf
Was put on the shelf
Because he could not spell "pie";
When his aunt, Mrs. Grace,
Saw his sorrowful face,
She could not help saying, "Oh, fie!"

And since Master Jelf
Was put on the shelf
Because he could not spell "pie,"
Let him stand there so grim,
And no more about him,
For I wish him a very good-bye!

WHY MAY NOT I LOVE JOHNNY?

Johnny shall have a new bonnet,
And Johnny shall go to the fair,
And Johnny shall have a blue ribbon
To tie up his bonny brown hair.

And why may not I love Johnny?
And why may not Johnny love me?
And why may not I love Johnny
As well as another body?

And here's a leg for a stocking,
And here's a foot for a shoe,
And he has a kiss for his daddy,
And two for his mammy, I trow.

And why may not I love Johnny?
And why may not Johnny love me?
And why may not I love Johnny
As well as another body?

JACK SPRAT

JACK SPRAT

Jack Sprat
Could eat no fat,
His wife could eat no lean;
And so,
Betwixt them both,
They licked the platter clean.

HUSH-A-BYE

Hush-a-bye, baby,
Daddy is near;
Mamma is a lady,
And that's very clear.

DAFFODILS

Daffy-down-dilly has come to town
In a yellow petticoat and a green
    gown.

THE GIRL IN THE LANE

The girl in the lane, that couldn't
    speak plain,
Cried, "Gobble, gobble, gobble":
The man on the hill that couldn't
    stand still,
Went hobble, hobble, hobble.

HUSH-A-BYE

Hush-a-bye, baby, lie still with thy
    daddy,
Thy mammy has gone to the mill,
To get some meal to bake a cake,
So pray, my dear baby, lie still.

NANCY DAWSON

Nancy Dawson was so fine
She wouldn't get up to serve the
     swine;
She lies in bed till eight or nine,
So it's Oh, poor Nancy
     Dawson.

And do ye ken Nancy Dawson,
     honey?
The wife who sells the barley, honey?
She won't get up to feed her swine,
And do ye ken Nancy Dawson,
     honey?

Harry the Great

So vast is the prowess of Harry the
　　Great,
He'll pluck a hair from the pale-faced
　　moon;
Or a lion familiarly take by the tooth,
And lead him about as you lead a
　　baboon.
All princes and potentates under the
　　sun,
Through fear into corners and holes
　　away run;
While nor dangers nor dread his
　　swift progress retards,
For he deals about kingdoms as we
　　do our cards.

The Alphabet

A, B, C, and D,
Pray, playmates agree.
E, F, and G,
Well, so it shall be.
J, K, and L,
In peace we will dwell.
M, N, and O,
To play let us go.
P, Q, R, and S,
Love may we possess.
W, X, and Y,
Will not quarrel or die.
Z, and ampersand,
Go to school at command.

Dance to Your Daddie

Dance to your daddie,
My bonnie laddie;
Dance to your daddie, my bonnie
    lamb;
You shall get a fishy,
On a little dishy;
You shall get a fishy, when the boat
    comes home.

One Misty Moisty Morning

One misty moisty morning,
When cloudy was the weather,
I chanced to meet an old man,
Clothed all in leather.
He began to compliment
And I began to grin.
How do you do? And how do you
    do?
And how do you do again?

Robin Hood and Little John

Robin Hood, Robin Hood,
Is in the mickle wood!
Little John, Little John,
He to the town is gone.

Robin Hood, Robin Hood,
Telling his beads,
All in the greenwood
Among the green weeds.

Little John, Little John,
If he comes no more,
Robin Hood, Robin Hood,
We shall fret full sore!

Rain

Rain, rain, go to Spain,
And never come back again.

ROBIN HOOD

THE ROBINS

A robin and a robin's son
Once went to town to buy a bun.
They couldn't decide on plum or
    plain,
And so they went back home again.

THE OLD MAN

There was an old man
In a velvet coat,
He kissed a maid
And gave her a groat.
The groat it was crack'd
And would not go,—
Ah, old man, do you serve me so?

THE OLD WOMAN FROM FRANCE

There came an old woman from
    France
Who taught grown-up children to
    dance;
But they were so stiff,
She sent them home in a sniff,
This sprightly old woman from
    France.

TEETH AND GUMS

Thirty white horses upon a red hill,
Now they tramp, now they champ,
    now they stand still.

T'OTHER LITTLE TUNE

I won't be my father's Jack,
I won't be my father's Jill;
I will be the fiddler's wife,
And have music when I will.
T'other little tune,
T'other little tune,
Prithee, Love, play me
T'other little tune.

MY KITTEN

Hey, my kitten, my kitten,
And hey, my kitten, my deary!
Such a sweet pet as this
Was neither far nor neary.

IF ALL THE SEAS WERE ONE SEA

If all the seas were one sea,
What a *great* sea that would be!
And if all the trees were one tree,
What a *great* tree that would be!
And if all the axes were one axe,
What a *great* axe that would be!
And if all the men were one man,
What a *great* man he would be!
And if the *great* man took the *great*
     axe,
And cut down the *great* tree,
And let it fall into the *great* sea,
What a splish splash *that* would be!

HERE SITS THE LORD MAYOR

Forehead, Eyes, Cheeks, Nose, Mouth, and Chin

Here sits the Lord Mayor,
Here sit his two men,
Here sits the cock,
Here sits the hen,
Here sit the little chickens,
Here they run in.
Chin-chopper, chin-chopper,
     chin-chopper, chin!

Two Pigeons

I had two pigeons bright and gay,
They flew from me the other day.
What was the reason they did go?
I cannot tell, for I do not know.

Pancake Day

Great A, little a,
This is pancake day;
Toss the ball high,
Throw the ball low,
Those that come after
May sing heigh-ho!

A Plum Pudding

Flour of England, fruit of Spain,
Met together in a shower of rain;
Put in a bag tied round with a string;
If you'll tell me this riddle,
I'll give you a ring.

A SURE TEST

If you are to be a gentleman,
As I suppose you'll be,
You'll neither laugh nor smile,
For a tickling of the knee.

LOCK AND KEY

"I am a gold lock."
"I am a gold key."
"I am a silver lock."
"I am a silver key."
"I am a brass lock."
"I am a brass key."
"I am a lead lock."
"I am a lead key."
"I am a don lock."
"I am a don key!"

THE LION AND THE UNICORN

The Lion and the Unicorn were
fighting for the crown,
The Lion beat the Unicorn all
around the town.
Some gave them white bread, and
some gave them brown,
Some gave them plum-cake, and sent
them out of town.

THE MERCHANTS OF LONDON

Hey diddle dinkety poppety pet,
The merchants of London they wear
scarlet,
Silk in the collar and gold in the
hem,
So merrily march the merchant men.

I'LL TELL YOU A STORY

I'll tell you a story
About Jack-a-Nory:
And now my story's begun.
I'll tell you another
About his brother:
And now my story is done.

A STRANGE OLD WOMAN

There was an old woman, and what
    do you think?
She lived upon nothing but victuals
    and drink;
Victuals and drink were the chief of
    her diet,
And yet this old woman could never
    be quiet.

I HAD A LITTLE HUSBAND

I had a little husband no bigger than
    my thumb,
I put him in a pint pot, and there
    I bid him drum,
I bought a little handkerchief to wipe
    his little nose,
And a pair of little garters to tie his
    little hose.

TO BABYLON

How many miles is it to Babylon?—
Threescore miles and ten.
Can I get there by candle-light?—
Yes, and back again.
If your heels are nimble and light,
You may get there by candle-light.

BAA, BAA, BLACK SHEEP

Baa, baa, black sheep,
Have you any wool?
Yes, marry, have I,
Three bags full;

One for my master,
One for my dame,
But none for the little boy
Who cries in the lane.

LITTLE FRED

When little Fred went to bed,
He always said his prayers;
He kissed mamma, and then papa,
And straightway went upstairs.

SLEEP, BABY, SLEEP

Sleep, baby, sleep,
Our cottage vale is deep:
The little lamb is on the green,
With woolly fleece so soft and clean—
Sleep, baby, sleep.

Sleep, baby, sleep,
Down where the woodbines creep;
Be always like the lamb so mild,
A kind, and sweet, and gentle child.
Sleep, baby, sleep.

CRY, BABY

Cry, baby, cry,
Put your finger in your eye,
And tell your mother it wasn't I.

BAA, BAA, BLACK SHEEP

THE CAT AND THE FIDDLE

Hey, diddle, diddle!
The cat and the fiddle,
The cow jumped over the moon;
The little dog laughed
To see such sport,
And the dish ran away with the spoon.

DOCTOR FELL

I do not like thee, Doctor Fell;
The reason why I cannot tell;
But this I know, and know full well,
I do not like thee, Doctor Fell!

A COUNTING-OUT RHYME

Hickery, dickery, 6 and 7,
Alabone, Crackabone, 10 and 11,
Spin, spun, muskidun,
Twiddle 'em, twaddle 'em, 21.

JACK AND HIS FIDDLE

"Jacky, come and give me thy fiddle,
If ever thou mean to thrive."
"Nay, I'll not give my fiddle
To any man alive.

"If I should give my fiddle,
They'll think that I've gone mad;
For many a joyous day
My fiddle and I have had."

BUTTONS

Buttons, a farthing a pair!
Come, who will buy them of me?
They're round and sound and pretty,
And fit for girls of the city.
Come, who will buy them of me?
Buttons, a farthing a pair!

HOT BOILED BEANS

Ladies and gentlemen come to
supper—
Hot boiled beans and very good
butter.

When the pie was opened
The birds began to sing;
Was not that a dainty dish
To set before the king?

The king was in his counting-
  house,
Counting out his money;
The queen was in the parlor,
Eating bread and honey.

The maid was in the garden,
Hanging out the clothes;
When down came a blackbird
And snapped off her nose.

LITTLE PUSSY

I like little Pussy,
Her coat is so warm,
And if I don't hurt her
She'll do me no harm;
So I'll not pull her tail,
Nor drive her away,
But Pussy and I
Very gently will play.

SING A SONG
OF SIXPENCE

Sing a song of sixpence,
A pocket full of rye;
Four-and-twenty blackbirds
Baked in a pie!

SING A SONG OF SIXPENCE

TOMMY TITTLEMOUSE

Little Tommy Tittlemouse
Lived in a little house;
He caught fishes
In other men's ditches.

THE DERBY RAM

As I was going to Derby all on a
market-day,
I met the finest ram, sir, that ever
was fed upon hay;
Upon hay, upon hay, upon hay;
I met the finest ram, sir, that ever
was fed upon hay.

This ram was fat behind, sir; this
ram was fat before;
This ram was ten yards round, sir;
indeed, he was no more;
No more, no more, no more;

This ram was ten yards round, sir;
indeed, he was no more.

The horns that grew on his head, sir,
they were so wondrous high,
As I've been plainly told, sir, they
reached up to the sky.
The sky, the sky, the sky;
As I've been plainly told, sir, they
reached up to the sky.

The tail that grew from his back, sir,
was six yards and an ell;
And it was sent to Derby to toll the
market bell;
The bell, the bell, the bell;
And it was sent to Derby to toll the
market bell.

THE HOBBY-HORSE

I had a little hobby-horse,
And it was dapple gray;
Its head was made of pea-straw,
Its tail was made of hay.

I sold it to an old woman
For a copper groat;
And I'll not sing my song again
Without another coat.

THE MULBERRY BUSH

Here we go round the mulberry bush,
The mulberry bush, the mulberry bush,
Here we go round the mulberry bush,
On a cold and frosty morning.

This is the way we wash our hands,
Wash our hands, wash our hands,
This is the way we wash our hands,
On a cold and frosty morning.

This is the way we wash our clothes,
Wash our clothes, wash our clothes,
This is the way we wash our clothes,
On a cold and frosty morning.

This is the way we go to school,
Go to school, go to school,
This is the way we go to school,
On a cold and frosty morning.

This is the way we come out of school,
Come out of school, come out of
    school,
This is the way we come out of school,
On a cold and frosty morning.

YOUNG LAMBS TO SELL

If I'd as much money as I could tell,
I never would cry young lambs to sell;
Young lambs to sell, young lambs
    to sell;
I never would cry young lambs to sell.

OLD WOMAN, OLD WOMAN

There was an old woman tossed in
    a basket,
Seventeen times as high as the moon;
But where she was going no mortal
    could tell,
For under her arm she carried a
    broom.

"Old woman, old woman, old
    woman," said I,
"Whither, oh whither, oh whither
    so high?"
"To sweep the cobwebs from the sky;
And I'll be with you by-and-by."

BOY AND THE SPARROW

A little cock-sparrow sat on a green
    tree,
And he chirruped, he chirruped, so
    merry was he;
A naughty boy came with his wee
    bow and arrow,
Determined to shoot this little cock-
    sparrow.
"This little cock-sparrow shall make
    me a stew,
And his giblets shall make me a little
    pie, too."
"Oh, no," says the sparrow "I won't
    make a stew."
So he flapped his wings and away he
    flew.

THE FIRST OF MAY

The fair maid who, the first of May,
Goes to the fields at break of day,
And washes in dew from the
    hawthorn-tree,
Will ever after handsome be.

THE OLD WOMAN TOSSED IN A BASKET

SULKY SUE

Here's Sulky Sue,
What shall we do?
Turn her face to the wall
Till she comes to.

THE HOUSE THAT
JACK BUILT

This is the house that Jack built.

This is the malt
That lay in the house that Jack built.

This is the rat,
That ate the malt
That lay in the house that Jack built.

This is the cat,
That killed the rat,
That ate the malt
That lay in the house that Jack built.

This is the dog,
That worried the cat,
That killed the rat,
That ate the malt
That lay in the house that Jack built.

This is the cow with the crumpled
    horn,
That tossed the dog,
That worried the cat,
That killed the rat,
That ate the malt
That lay in the house that Jack built.

This is the maiden all forlorn,
That milked the cow with the
    crumpled horn,
That tossed the dog,
That worried the cat,
That killed the rat,
That ate the malt
That lay in the house that Jack built.

This is the man all tattered and torn,
That kissed the maiden all forlorn,
That milked the cow with the
    crumpled horn,
That tossed the dog,
That worried the cat,
That killed the rat,
That ate the malt
That lay in the house that Jack built.

This is the priest all shaven and shorn,
That married the man all tattered
    and torn,
That kissed the maiden all forlorn,
That milked the cow with the
    crumpled horn,
That tossed the dog,
That worried the cat,
That killed the rat,
That ate the malt
That lay in the house that Jack built.

This is the cock that crowed in the
    morn,
That waked the priest all shaven and
    shorn,
That married the man all tattered
    and torn,
That kissed the maiden all forlorn,
That milked the cow with the
    crumpled horn,
That tossed the dog,
That worried the cat,
That killed the rat,
That ate the malt
That lay in the house that Jack built.

This is the farmer sowing the corn,
That kept the cock that crowed in the
    morn,
That waked the priest all shaven and
    shorn,

That married the man all tattered
    and torn,
That kissed the maiden all forlorn,
That milked the cow with the
    crumpled horn,
That tossed the dog,
That worried the cat,
That killed the rat,
That ate the malt
That lay in the house that Jack built.

SATURDAY, SUNDAY

On Saturday night
Shall be all my care
To powder my locks
And curl my hair.

On Sunday morning
My love will come in,
When he will marry me
With a gold ring.

THE OLD WOMAN AND THE PEDLAR

LITTLE JENNY WREN

Little Jenny Wren fell sick,
Upon a time;
In came Robin Redbreast
And brought her cake and wine.

"Eat well of my cake, Jenny,
Drink well of my wine."
"Thank you, Robin, kindly,
You shall be mine."

Jenny she got well,
And stood upon her feet,
And told Robin plainly
She loved him not a bit.

Robin being angry,
Hopped upon a twig,
Saying, "Out upon you! Fie upon you!
Bold-faced jig!"

THE OLD WOMAN AND
THE PEDLAR

There was an old woman, as I've
heard tell,
She went to market her eggs for to
sell;
She went to market all on a market-
day,
And she fell asleep on the King's
highway.

There came by a pedlar whose name
was Stout,

He cut her petticoats all round
about;
He cut her petticoats up to the
knees,
Which made the old woman to
shiver and freeze.

When the little old woman first did
wake,
She began to shiver and she began to
shake;
She began to wonder and she began
to cry,
"Lauk a mercy on me, this can't
be I!

"But if it be I, as I hope it be,
I've a little dog at home, and he'll
  know me;
If it be I, he'll wag his little tail,
And if it be not I, he'll loudly bark
  and wail."

Home went the little woman all in
  the dark;
Up got the little dog, and he began
  to bark;
He began to bark, so she began to
  cry,
"Lauk a mercy on me, this is none
  of I!"

BOBBY SNOOKS

Little Bobby Snooks was fond of
  his books,
And loved by his usher and master;
But naughty Jack Spry, he got a
  black eye,
And carries his nose in a plaster.

THE LITTLE MOPPET

I had a little moppet,
I put it in my pocket,
And fed it with corn and hay.
There came a proud beggar,
And swore he should have her,
And stole my little moppet away.

I Saw a Ship A-Sailing

I saw a ship a-sailing,
A-sailing on the sea;
And, oh! it was all laden
With pretty things for thee!

There were comfits in the cabin,
And apples in the hold;
The sails were made of silk,
And the masts were made of gold.

The four-and-twenty sailors
That stood between the decks,
Were four-and-twenty white mice
With chains about their necks.

The captain was a duck,
With a packet on his back;
And when the ship began to move,
The captain said, "Quack! Quack!"

A Walnut

As soft as silk, as white as milk,
As bitter as gall, a strong wall,
And a green coat covers me all.

The Man in the Moon

The Man in the Moon came
    tumbling down,
And asked the way to Norwich;
He went by the south, and burnt his
    mouth
With eating cold pease porridge.

One, He Loves

One, he loves; two, he loves;
Three, he loves, they say;
Four, he loves with all his heart;
Five, he casts away.
Six, he loves; seven, she loves;
Eight, they both love.
Nine, he comes; ten, he tarries;
Eleven, he courts; twelve, he marries.

Bat, Bat

Bat, bat,
Come under my hat,
And I'll give you a slice of bacon;
And when I bake
I'll give you a cake
If I am not mistaken.

HARK! HARK! THE DOGS DO BARK!

MY LOVE

Saw ye aught of my love a-coming
    from the market?
A peck of meal upon her back,
A babby in her basket;
Saw ye aught of my love a-coming
    from the market?

THE MAN OF BOMBAY

There was a fat man of Bombay,
Who was smoking one sunshiny
    day;
When a bird called a snipe
Flew away with his pipe,
Which vexed the fat man of
    Bombay.

HARK! HARK!

Hark! hark! the dogs do bark!
Beggars are coming to town:
Some in jags, and some in rags,
And some in velvet gown.

THE HART

The hart he loves the high wood,
The hare she loves the hill;
The Knight he loves his bright
    sword,
The Lady—loves her will.

MY MAID MARY

My maid Mary she minds the dairy,
While I go a-hoeing and mowing
    each morn;
Gaily run the reel and the little
    spinning wheel.
While I am singing and mowing my
    corn.

A DIFFICULT RHYME

What is the rhyme for porringer?
The king he had a daughter fair,
And gave the Prince of Orange her.

POOR OLD ROBINSON CRUSOE!

Poor old Robinson Crusoe!
Poor old Robinson Crusoe!
They made him a coat
Of an old Nanny goat.
I wonder why they should do so!
With a ring-a-ting-tang,
And a ring-a-ting-tang,
Poor old Robinson Crusoe!

A SIEVE

A riddle, a riddle, as I suppose,
A hundred eyes and never a nose!

PRETTY JOHN WATTS

Pretty John Watts,
We are troubled with rats,
Will you drive them out of the
	house?
We have mice, too, in plenty,
That feast in the pantry,
But let them stay
And nibble away,
What harm in a little brown mouse?

GOOD ADVICE

Come when you're called,
Do what you're bid,
Shut the door after you,
And never be chid.

I LOVE SIXPENCE

I love sixpence, a jolly, jolly
	sixpence,
I love sixpence as my life;
I spent a penny of it, I spent a penny
	of it,
I took a penny home to my wife.

Oh, my little fourpence, a jolly, jolly
	fourpence,
I love fourpence as my life;
I spent twopence of it, I spent
	twopence of it,
And I took twopence home to
	my wife.

BYE, BABY BUNTING

Bye, baby bunting,
Father's gone a-hunting,
Mother's gone a-milking,
Sister's gone a-silking,
And brother's gone to buy a skin
To wrap the baby bunting in.

TOM, TOM, THE PIPER'S SON

Tom, Tom, the piper's son,
Stole a pig, and away he run,
The pig was eat,
And Tom was beat,
And Tom ran crying down the street.

COMICAL FOLK

In a cottage in Fife
Lived a man and his wife
Who, believe me, were comical folk;
For, to people's surprise,
They both saw with their eyes,
And their tongues moved whenever
    they spoke!

When they were asleep,
I'm told, that to keep
Their eyes open they could not
    contrive;
They both walked on their feet,
And 'twas thought what they eat
Helped, with drinking, to keep them
    alive!

COCK-CROW

Cocks crow in the morn
To tell us to rise,
And he who lies late
Will never be wise;
For early to bed
And early to rise,
Is the way to be healthy
And wealthy and wise.

TOMMY SNOOKS

As Tommy Snooks and Bessy Brooks
Were walking out one Sunday,
Says Tommy Snooks to Bessy
    Brooks,
"Wilt marry me on Monday?"

COCK-CROW

THE THREE SONS

There was an old woman had three
    sons,
Jerry and James and John,
Jerry was hanged, James was
    drowned,
John was lost and never was found;
And there was an end of her three
    sons,
Jerry and James and John!

THE BLACKSMITH

"Robert Barnes, my fellow fine,
Can you shoe this horse of mine?"
"Yes, good sir, that I can,
As well as any other man;
There's a nail, and there's a prod,
Now, good sir, your horse is shod."

TWO GRAY KITS

The two gray kits,
And the gray kits' mother,
All went over
The bridge together.

The bridge broke down,
They all fell in;
"May the rats go with you,"
Says Tom Bolin.

ONE, TWO, BUCKLE MY SHOE

One, two,
Buckle my shoe;
Three, four,
Knock at the door;
Five, six,
Pick up sticks;
Seven, eight,
Lay them straight;
Nine, ten,
A good, fat hen;
Eleven, twelve,
Dig and delve;
Thirteen, fourteen,
Maids a-courting;
Fifteen, sixteen,
Maids in the kitchen;
Seventeen, eighteen,
Maids a-waiting;
Nineteen, twenty,
My plate's empty.

COCK-A-DOODLE-DO!

Cock-a-doodle-do!
My dame has lost her shoe,
My master's lost his fiddle-stick
And knows not what to do.

Cock-a-doodle-do!
What is my dame to do?
Till master finds his fiddle-stick,
She'll dance without her shoe.

PAIRS OR PEARS

Twelve pairs hanging high,
Twelve knights riding by,
Each knight took a pear,
And yet left a dozen there.

BELLEISLE

At the siege of Belleisle
I was there all the while,
All the while, all the while,
At the siege of Belleisle.

DAPPLE-GRAY

OLD KING COLE

Old King Cole
Was a merry old soul,
And a merry old soul was he;
He called for his pipe,
And he called for his bowl,
And he called for his fiddlers three!
And every fiddler, he had a fine
    fiddle,
And a very fine fiddle had he.
"Twee tweedle dee, tweedle dee,"
    went the fiddlers.
Oh, there's none so rare
As can compare
With King Cole and his fiddlers
    three.

SEE, SEE

See, see! What shall I see?
A horse's head where his tail should
    be.

DAPPLE-GRAY

I had a little pony,
His name was Dapple-Gray,
I lent him to a lady,
To ride a mile away.
She whipped him, she slashed him,
She rode him through the mire;
I would not lend my pony now
For all the lady's hire.

A WELL

As round as an apple, as deep as
    a cup,
And all the king's horses can't fill
    it up.

COFFEE AND TEA

Molly, my sister, and I fell out,
And what do you think it was
    all about?
She loved coffee and I loved tea,
And that was the reason we couldn't
    agree.

PUSSY-CAT MEW

Pussy-cat Mew jumped over a coal,
And in her best petticoat burnt a
    great hole.
Poor Pussy's weeping, she'll have no
    more milk
Until her best petticoat's mended
    with silk.

A Cock and Bull Story

The cock's on the housetop blowing
  his horn;
The bull's in the barn a-threshing of
  corn;
The maids in the meadows are
  making of hay;
The ducks in the river are swimming
  away.

For Baby

You shall have an apple,
You shall have a plum,
You shall have a rattle,
When papa comes home.

The Little Girl with
  a Curl

There was a little girl who had a
  little curl
Right in the middle of her forehead;
When she was good, she was very,
  very good,
And when she was bad she was
  horrid.

Dreams

Friday night's dream, on Saturday
  told,
Is sure to come true, be it never
  so old.

OVER THE WATER

Over the water, and over the sea,
And over the water to Charley,
I'll have none of your nasty beef,
Nor I'll have none of your barley;
But I'll have some of your very best
    flour
To make a white cake for my
    Charley.

CANDLE-SAVING

To make your candles last for aye,
You wives and maids give ear-O!
To put them out's the only way,
Says honest John Boldero.

MYSELF

As I walked by myself,
And talked to myself,
Myself said unto me:
"Look to thyself,
Take care of thyself,
For nobody cares for thee."

I answered myself,
And said to myself
In the selfsame repartee:
"Look to thyself,
Or not look to thyself,
The selfsame thing will be."

LADYBIRD

FEARS AND TEARS

Tommy's tears and Mary's fears
Will mark them old before their years.

THE KILKENNY CATS

There were once two cats of
    Kilkenny.
Each thought there was one cat too
    many;
So they fought and they fit,
And they scratched and they bit,
Till, excepting their nails,
And the tips of their tails,
Instead of two cats, there weren't
    any.

OLD GRIMES

Old Grimes is dead, that good old
    man,
We ne'er shall see him more;
He used to wear a long brown coat
All buttoned down before.

A WEEK OF BIRTHDAYS

Monday's child is fair of face,
Tuesday's child is full of grace,
Wednesday's child is full of woe,
Thursday's child has far to go,
Friday's child is loving and giving,
Saturday's child works hard for its
    living,
But the child that's born on the
    Sabbath day
Is bonny and blithe, and good
    and gay.

A CHIMNEY

Black within and red without;
Four corners round about.

LADYBIRD

Ladybird, ladybird, fly away home!
Your house is on fire, your children
    all gone,
All but one, and her name is Ann,
And she crept under the pudding
    pan.

THE MAN WHO HAD NAUGHT

There was a man and he had naught,
And robbers came to rob him;
He crept up to the chimney pot,
And then they thought they had
    him.
But he got down on t'other side,
And then they could not find him;
He ran fourteen miles in fifteen days,
And never looked behind him.

THE TAILORS AND
THE SNAIL

Four and Twenty tailors
Went to kill a snail;
The best man among them
Durst not touch her tail;
She put out her horns
Like a little Kyloe cow.
Run, tailors, run, or
She'll kill you all e'en now.

AROUND THE GREEN
GRAVEL

Around the green gravel the grass
    grows green,
And all the pretty maids are plain
    to be seen;
Wash them with milk, and clothe
    them with silk,
And write their names with a pen and
    ink.

INTERY, MINTERY

Intery, mintery, cutery corn,
Apple seed and apple thorn;
Wire, brier, limber-lock,
Five geese in a flock,
Sit and sing by a spring,
O-u-t, and in again.

CAESAR'S SONG

Bow-wow-wow!
Whose dog art thou?
Little Tom Tinker's dog,
Bow-wow-wow!

As I Was Going Along

As I was going along, along,
A-singing a comical song, song, song,
The lane that I went was so long, long,
    long,
And the song that I sang was so long,
    long, long,
And so I went singing along.

Hector Protector

Hector Protector was dressed all in
    green;
Hector Protector was sent to the Queen.
The Queen did not like him,
No more did the King;
So Hector Protector was sent back
    again.

Billy, Billy

"Billy, Billy, come and play,
While the sun shines bright as day."

"Yes, my Polly, so I will,
For I love to please you still."

"Billy, Billy, have you seen
Sam and Betsy on the green?"

"Yes, my Poll, I saw them pass,
Skipping o'er the new-mown grass."

"Billy, Billy, come along,
And I will sing a pretty song."

Rock-a-Bye, Baby

Rock-a-bye, baby, thy cradle is
    green;
Father's a nobleman, mother's a
    queen;
And Betty's a lady, and wears a gold
    ring;
And Johnny's a drummer, and
    drums for the king.

The Man in the Wilderness

The man in the wilderness
    Asked me
How many strawberries
Grew in the sea.
I answered him
As I thought good,
As many as red herrings
Grew in the wood.

MARY, MARY, QUITE CONTRARY

Mary, Mary, quite contrary,
How does your garden grow?
Silver bells and cockle-shells,
And pretty maids all of a row.

BESSY BELL AND MARY GRAY

Bessy Bell and Mary Gray,
They were two bonny lasses;
They built their house upon
the lea,
And covered it with rushes.

Bessy kept the garden gate,
And Mary kept the pantry;
Bessy always had to wait,
While Mary lived in plenty.

LITTLE JACK HORNER

Little Jack Horner
Sat in the corner,
Eating of Christmas pie:
He put in his thumb,
And pulled out a plum,
And said, "What a good boy am I!"

THE BIRD SCARER

Away, birds, away!
Take a little and leave a little,
And do not come again;
For if you do,
I will shoot you through,
And there will be an end of you.

MARY, MARY, QUITE CONTRARY

NEEDLES AND PINS

Needles and pins, needles and
    pins,
When a man marries his trouble
    begins.

PUSSY-CAT AND THE
DUMPLINGS

Pussy-cat ate the dumplings, the
    dumplings,
Pussy-cat ate the dumplings.
Mamma stood by, and cried,
    "Oh, fie!
Why did you eat the dumplings?"

DANCE, THUMBKIN, DANCE

Dance, Thumbkin, dance;
(keep the thumb in motion)
Dance, ye merrymen, everyone.
(all the fingers in motion)
For Thumbkin, he can dance alone,
(the thumb alone moving)
Thumbkin, he can dance alone.
(the thumb alone moving)
Dance, Foreman, dance,
(the first finger moving)
Dance, ye merrymen, everyone.
(all moving)
But Foreman, he can dance alone,
(the first finger moving)
Foreman, he can dance alone.
(the first finger moving)
Dance, Longman, dance,
(the second finger moving)
Dance, ye merrymen, everyone.
(all moving)
For Longman, he can dance alone,
(the second finger moving)
Longman, he can dance alone.
(the second finger moving)
Dance, Ringman, dance,
(the third finger moving)
Dance, ye merrymen, dance.
(all moving)
But Ringman cannot dance alone,
(the third finger moving)
Ringman, he cannot dance alone.
(the third finger moving)
Dance, Littleman, dance,
(the fourth finger moving)
Dance, ye merrymen, dance.
(all moving)
But Littleman, he can dance alone,
(the fourth finger moving)
Littleman, he can dance alone.
(the fourth finger moving)

THE LITTLE BIRD

Once I saw a little bird
Come hop, hop, hop;
So I cried, "Little bird,
Will you stop, stop, stop?"

And was going to the window
To say, "How do you do?"
But he shook his little tail,
And far away he flew.

BIRDS OF A FEATHER

Birds of a feather flock together,
And so will pigs and swine;
Rats and mice will have their choice,
And so will I have mine.

MARY'S CANARY

Mary had a pretty bird,
Feathers bright and yellow,
Slender legs—upon my word,
He was a pretty fellow!

The sweetest note he always sung
Which much delighted Mary.
She often, where the cage was hung,
Sat hearing her canary.

THE DUSTY MILLER

Margaret wrote a letter,
Sealed it with her finger,
Threw it in the dam
For the dusty miller.
Dusty was his coat,
Dusty was the siller,
Dusty was the kiss
I'd from the dusty miller.
If I had my pockets
Full of gold and siller,
I would give it all
To my dusty miller.

A STAR

Higher than a house, higher than a
    tree.
Oh! whatever can that be?

THE GREEDY MAN

The greedy man is he who sits
And bites bits out of plates,
Or else takes up an almanac
And gobbles all the dates.

THE TEN O'CLOCK SCHOLAR

A diller, a dollar, a ten o'clock
    scholar!
What makes you come so soon?
You used to come at ten o'clock,
But now you come at noon.

THE TEN O'CLOCK SCHOLAR

COCK-A-DOODLE DO

Oh, my pretty cock, oh, my handsome cock,
I pray you, do not crow before day,
And your comb shall be made of the very
     beaten gold,
And your wings of the silver so gray.

AN ICICLE

Lives in winter,
Dies in summer,
And grows with its roots upward!

A SHIP'S NAIL

Over the water,
And under the water,
And always with its head down.

THE OLD WOMAN OF LEEDS

There was an old woman of Leeds,
Who spent all her time in good
    deeds;
She worked for the poor
Till her fingers were sore,
This pious old woman of Leeds!

THE BOY IN THE BARN

A little boy went into a barn,
And lay down on some hay.
An owl came out, and flew about,
And the little boy ran away.

SUNSHINE

Hick-a-more, Hack-a-more,
On the King's kitchen door;
All the King's horses,
And all the King's men,
Couldn't drive Hick-a-more,
    Hack-a-more,
Off the King's kitchen door.

WILLY, WILLY

Willy, Willy Wilkin
Kissed the maids a-milking,
Fa, la, la!
And with his merry daffing
He set them all a-laughing,
Ha, ha, ha!

THE QUARREL

My little old man and I fell out;
I'll tell you what 'twas all about,—
I had money and he had none,
And that's the way the noise begun.

THE PUMPKIN-EATER

Peter, Peter, pumpkin-eater,
Had a wife and couldn't keep her;
He put her in a pumpkin shell,
And there he kept her very well.

TONGS

Long legs, crooked thighs,
Little head, and no eyes.

JACK JINGLE

Little Jack Jingle,
He used to live single;
But when he got tired of this kind
   of life,
He left off being single and lived
   with his wife.
Now what do you think of little
   Jack Jingle?
Before he was married he used to
   live single.

PETER, PETER, PUMPKIN-EATER

THAT'S ALL

There was an old woman sat
      spinning,
And that's the first beginning;

She had a calf,
And that's half;

She took it by the tail,
And threw it over the wall,
And that's all!

SHOEING

Shoe the colt,
Shoe the colt,
Shoe the wild mare;
Here a nail,
There a nail,
Yet she goes bare.

BETTY BLUE

Little Betty Blue
Lost her holiday shoe;
What shall little Betty do?
Give her another
To match the other
And then she'll walk upon two.

BEDTIME

The Man in the Moon looked
    out of the moon,
Looked out of the moon
    and said,
"'Tis time for all children on
    the earth
To think about getting
    to bed!"

DANCE, LITTLE BABY

Dance, little Baby, dance up high!
Never mind, Baby, Mother is by.
Crow and caper, caper and crow,
There, little Baby, there you go!
Up to the ceiling, down to the
    ground,
Backwards and forwards, round and
    round;
Dance, little Baby and Mother will
    sing,
With the merry coral, ding, ding,
    ding!

MY LITTLE MAID

High diddle doubt, my candle's out
My little maid is not at home;
Saddle my hog and bridle
    my dog,
And fetch my little maid home.

FOR WANT OF A NAIL

For want of a nail, the shoe was lost;
For want of the shoe, the horse
    was lost;
For want of the horse, the rider
    was lost;
For want of the rider, the battle
    was lost;
For want of the battle, the kingdom
    was lost,
And all for the want of a horseshoe
    nail.

THE CROOKED SIXPENCE

There was a crooked man, and
    he went a crooked mile,
He found a crooked sixpence
    beside a crooked stile;
He bought a crooked cat, which
    caught a crooked mouse,
And they all lived together in a
    little crooked house.

THIS IS THE WAY

This is the way the ladies ride,
Tri, tre, tre, tree,
Tri, tre, tre, tree!
This is the way the ladies ride,
Tri, tre, tre, tre, tri-tre-tre-tree!

This is the way the
    gentlemen ride,
Gallop-a-trot,
Gallop-a-trot!
This is the way the
    gentlemen ride,
Gallop-a-gallop-a-trot!

This is the way the
    farmers ride,
Hobbledy-hoy,
Hobbledy-hoy!
This is the way the
    farmers ride,
Hobbledy-hobbledy-hoy!

PEASE PORRIDGE

Pease porridge hot,
Pease porridge cold,
Pease porridge in the pot,
Nine days old.
Some like it hot,
Some like it cold,
Some like it in the pot,
Nine days old.

RING A RING O' ROSES

Ring a ring o' roses,
A pocketful of posies.
Tisha! Tisha!
We all fall down.

PEASE PORRIDGE HOT

DUCKS AND DRAKES

A duck and a drake,
And a halfpenny cake,
With a penny to pay the old baker.

A hop and a scotch
Is another notch,
Slitherum, slatherum, take her.

THE DONKEY

Donkey, donkey, old and gray,
Ope your mouth and gently bray;
Lift your ears and blow your horn,
To wake the world this sleepy morn.

IF

If all the world were apple pie,
And all the sea were ink,
And all the trees were bread
    and cheese,
What should we have for drink?

THE BELLS

"You owe me five shillings,"
Say the bells of St. Helen's.

"When will you pay me?"
Say the bells of Old Bailey.

"When I grow rich,"
Say the bells of Shoreditch.

"When will that be?"
Say the bells of Stepney.

"I do not know,"
Says the great Bell of Bow.

"Two sticks in an apple,"
Ring the bells of Whitechapel.

"Halfpence and farthings,"
Say the bells of St. Martin's.

"Kettles and pans,"
Say the bells of St. Ann's.

"Brickbats and tiles,"
Say the bells of St. Giles.

"Old shoes and slippers,"
Say the bells of St. Peter's.

"Pokers and tongs,"
Say the bells of St. John's.

LITTLE GIRL AND QUEEN

"Little girl, little girl, where have you
    been ?"
"Gathering roses to give to the
    Queen."
"Little girl, little girl, what gave
    she you?"
"She gave me a diamond as big as my
    shoe."

THE KING OF FRANCE

The King of France went up the hill,
With twenty thousand men;
The King of France came down the
    hill,
And ne'er went up again.

THE TARTS

PETER PIPER

Peter Piper picked a peck of pickled
    peppers;
A peck of pickled peppers Peter Piper
    picked.
If Peter Piper picked a peck of
    pickled peppers,
Where's the peck of pickled peppers
    Peter Piper picked?

ONE TO TEN

1, 2, 3, 4, 5!
I caught a hare alive;
6, 7, 8, 9, 10!
I let her go again.

AN EQUAL

Read my riddle, I pray.
What God never sees,
What the king seldom sees,
What we see every day.

THE TARTS

The Queen of Hearts,
She made some tarts,
All on a summer's day;
The Knave of Hearts,
He stole the tarts,
And took them clean away.

The King of Hearts
Called for the tarts,
And beat the Knave full sore;
The Knave of Hearts
Brought back the tarts,
And vowed he'd steal no more.

WHAT ARE LITTLE BOYS MADE OF?

What are little boys made of,
    made of?
What are little boys made of?
"Snaps and snails, and puppy-dogs'
    tails;
And that's what little boys are made
    of."

What are little girls made of,
    made of?
What are little girls made of?
"Sugar and spice, and all that's nice;
And that's what little girls are made
    of."

COME, LET'S TO BED

"To bed! To bed!"
Says Sleepy-head;
"Tarry awhile," says Slow;
"Put on the pan,"
Says Greedy Nan;
"We'll sup before we go."

LITTLE MAID

"Little maid, pretty maid, whither
    goest thou?"
"Down in the forest to milk
    my cow."
"Shall I go with thee?" "No, not
    now;
When I send for thee, then come
    thou."

I went into the woods and built
    me a kirk,
And all the birds of the air, they
    helped me to work.

The hawk with his long claws
    pulled down the stone,
The dove with her rough bill
    brought me them home.

The parrot was the clergyman,
    the peacock was the clerk,
The bullfinch played the organ,—
    we made merry work.

BANDY LEGS

As I was going to sell my eggs
I met a man with bandy legs,
Bandy legs and crooked toes;
I tripped up his heels, and he fell on
    his nose.

THE GIRL AND THE BIRDS

When I was a little girl, about seven
    years old,
I hadn't got a petticoat, to cover me
    from the cold.

So I went into Darlington, that
    pretty little town,
And there I bought a petticoat, a
    cloak, and a gown.

A PIG

As I went to Bonner,
I met a pig
Without a wig
Upon my word and honor.

JENNY WREN

As little Jenny Wren
Was sitting by her shed,
She waggled with her tail,
And nodded with her head.
She waggled with her tail,
And nodded with her head,
As little Jenny Wren
Was sitting by the shed.

LITTLE TOM TUCKER

Little Tom Tucker
Sings for his supper.
What shall he eat?
White bread and butter.
How will he cut it
Without e'er a knife?
How will he be married
Without e'er a wife?

LITTLE TOM TUCKER

WHERE ARE YOU GOING, MY PRETTY MAID?

"Where are you going, my pretty
    maid?"
"I'm going a-milking, sir," she said.
"May I go with you, my pretty
    maid?"
"You're kindly welcome sir,"
    she said.
"What is your father, my pretty
    maid?"
"My father's a farmer, sir," she said.
"What is your fortune, my pretty
    maid?"
"My face is my fortune, sir,"
    she said.
"Then I can't marry you, my pretty
    maid."
"Nobody asked you, sir," she said.

THE OLD WOMAN OF GLOUCESTER

There was an old woman of
    Gloucester,
Whose parrot two guineas it cost her,
But its tongue never ceasing,
Was vastly displeasing
To the talkative woman of
    Gloucester.

MULTIPLICATION IS VEXATION

Multiplication is vexation,
Division is as bad;
The Rule of Three doth puzzle me,
And Practice drives me mad.

LITTLE KING BOGGEN

Little King Boggen, he built a fine
    hall,
Pie-crust and pastry-crust, that was
    the wall;
The windows were made of black
    puddings and white,
And slated with pan-cakes,—you
    ne'er saw the like!

WHISTLE

"Whistle, daughter, whistle;
Whistle, daughter dear."
"I cannot whistle, mammy,
I cannot whistle clear."
"Whistle, daughter, whistle;
Whistle for a pound."
"I cannot whistle, mammy,
I cannot make a sound."

BELL HORSES

Bell horses, bell horses, what time
    of day?
One o'clock, two o'clock, three
    and away.

TAFFY

Taffy was a Welshman, Taffy was a
    thief,
Taffy came to my house and stole a
    piece of beef;
I went to Taffy's house, Taffy was not
    home;
Taffy came to my house and stole a
    marrow-bone.

I went to Taffy's house, Taffy was not
    in;
Taffy came to my house and stole a
    silver pin;
I went to Taffy's house, Taffy was in
    bed,
I took up the marrow-bone and flung
    it at his head.

YOUNG ROGER AND DOLLY

Young Roger came tapping at Dolly's
    window,
Thumpaty, thumpaty, thump!

He asked for admittance; she
    answered him "No!"
Frumpaty, frumpaty, frump!

"No, no, Roger, no! as you came you
    may go!"
Stumpaty, stumpaty, stump!

THE ROBIN

The north wind doth blow,
And we shall have snow,
And what will poor robin do then,
    Poor thing?
He'll sit in a barn,
And keep himself warm,
And hide his head under his wing,
    Poor thing!

THE OLD WOMAN
OF HARROW

There was an old woman of
    Harrow,
Who visited in a wheelbarrow;
And her servant before,
Knocked loud at each door,
To announce the old woman of
    Harrow.

YOUNG ROGER AND DOLLY

THE COACHMAN

Up at Piccadilly, oh!
The coachman takes his stand,
And when he meets a pretty girl
He takes her by the hand;
Whip away forever, oh!
Drive away so clever, oh!
All the way to Bristol, oh!
He drives her four-in-hand.

THERE WAS AN OLD WOMAN

There was an old woman who lived
   in a shoe.
She had so many children she didn't
   know what to do.
She gave them some broth without
   any bread.
She whipped them all soundly and
   put them to bed.

THE PIPER AND HIS COW

There was a piper had a cow,
And he had naught to give her;
He pulled out his pipes and played
   her a tune,
And bade the cow consider.

The cow considered very well,
And gave the piper a penny,
And bade him play the other tune,
"Corn rigs are bonny."

THE MAN OF DERBY

A little old man of Derby,
How do you think he served me?
He took away my bread and cheese,
And that is how he served me.

A Thorn

I went to the wood and got it;
I sat me down to look for it
And brought it home because
    I couldn't find it.

The Old Woman of Surrey

There was an old woman in Surrey,
Who was morn, noon, and night
    in a hurry;
Called her husband a fool,
Drove the children to school,
The worrying old woman of Surrey.

The Little Mouse

I have seen you, little mouse,
Running all about the house,
Through the hole your little eye
In the wainscot peeping sly,
Hoping soon some crumbs
    to steal,
To make quite a hearty meal.
Look before you venture out,
See if pussy is about.
If she's gone, you'll quickly run
To the larder for some fun;
Round about the dishes creep,
Taking into each a peep,
To choose the daintiest that's
    there,
Spoiling things you do
    not care.

BOY AND GIRL

There was a little boy and a little
    girl
Lived in an alley;
Says the little boy to the little
    girl,
"Shall I, oh, shall I?"
Says the little girl to the little
    boy,
"What shall we do?"
Says the little boy to the little
    girl,
"I will kiss you."

WHEN

When I was a bachelor
I lived by myself;
And all the bread and cheese I got
I laid up on the shelf.

The rats and the mice
They made such a strife,
I was forced to go to London
To buy me a wife.

The streets were so bad,
And the lanes were so narrow,
I was forced to bring my wife home
In a wheelbarrow.

The wheelbarrow broke,
And my wife had a fall;
Down came wheelbarrow,
Little wife and all.

WHEN I WAS A BACHELOR

SING, SING

Sing, sing, what shall
　　I sing?
Cat's run away with
　　the pudding-
　　string!
Do, do, what shall I
　　do?
The cat has bitten it
　　quite in two.

LONDON BRIDGE

London Bridge is broken down,
Dance over my Lady Lee;
London Bridge is broken down,
With a gay lady.

How shall we build it up again?
Dance over my Lady Lee;
How shall we build it up again?
With a gay lady.

Build it up with silver and gold,
Dance over my Lady Lee;
Build it up with silver and gold,
With a gay lady.

Silver and gold will be stole away,
Dance over my Lady Lee;
Silver and gold will be stole away,
With a gay lady.

Build it up with iron and steel,
Dance over my Lady Lee;
Build it up with iron and steel,
With a gay lady.

Iron and steel will bend and bow,
Dance over my Lady Lee;
Iron and steel will bend and bow,
With a gay lady.

Build it up with wood and clay,
Dance over my Lady Lee;
Build it up with wood and clay,
With a gay lady.

Wood and clay will wash away,
Dance over my Lady Lee;
Wood and clay will wash away,
With a gay lady.

Build it up with stone so strong,
Dance over my Lady Lee;
Huzza! 'twill last for ages long,
With a gay lady.

MARCH WINDS

March winds and April showers
Bring forth May flowers.

THE LOST SHOE

Doodle doodle doo,
The Princess lost her shoe:
Her Highness hopped,—
The fiddler stopped,
Not knowing what to do.

HOT CODLINS

There was a little woman, as I've
     been told,
Who was not very young, nor yet
     very old;
Now this little woman her living
     got
By selling codlins, hot, hot, hot!

THE BALLOON

"What is the news of the day,
Good neighbor, I pray?"
"They say the balloon
Is gone up to the moon!"

A CHERRY

As I went through the garden gap,
Who should I meet but Dick
     Redcap!
A stick in his hand, a stone in his
     throat,—
If you'll tell me this riddle, I'll give
     you a groat.

MARY'S LAMB

MILLER AND MOUSE

There was an old woman
Lived under a hill.
She put a mouse in a bag,
And sent it to mill.
The miller did swear,
By the point of his knife,
He never took toll
Of a mouse in his life!

A

Apple pie, pudding, and pancake,
All begins with A.

MARY'S LAMB

Mary had a little lamb,
Its fleece was white as snow;
And everywhere that Mary went
The lamb was sure to go.

He followed her to school one day;
Which was against the rule;
It made the children laugh and play
To see a lamb at school.

And so the teacher turned him out,
But still he lingered near,
And waited patiently about
Till Mary did appear.

Then he ran to her, and laid
His head upon her arm,
As if he said, "I'm not afraid,—
You'll keep me from all harm."

"What makes the lamb love
        Mary so?"
The eager children cry.
"Oh, Mary loves the lamb,
        you know,"
The teacher did reply.

And you each gentle animal
In confidence may bind,
And make it follow at your will,
If you are only kind.

WILLY BOY

"Willy boy, Willy boy, where are you
    going?
I will go with you, if that I may."
"I'm going to the meadow to see
    them a-mowing,
I'm going to help them to make the
    hay."

POLLY AND SUKEY

Polly, put the kettle on,
Polly, put the kettle on,
Polly, put the kettle on,
And let's drink tea.

Sukey, take it off again,
Sukey, take it off again,
Sukey, take it off again,
They're all gone away.

THE DEATH AND BURIAL OF POOR COCK ROBIN

Who killed Cock Robin?
"I," said the sparrow,
"With my little bow and arrow,
I killed Cock Robin."

Who saw him die?
"I," said the fly,
"With my little eye,
I saw him die."

Who caught his blood?
"I," said the fish,
"With my little dish,
I caught his blood."

Who'll make his shroud?
"I," said the beetle,
"With my thread and needle,
I'll make his shroud."

Who'll carry the torch?
"I," said the linnet,
"I'll come in a minute,
I'll carry the torch."

Who'll be the clerk?
"I," said the lark,
"If it's not in the dark,
I'll be the clerk."

Who'll dig his grave?
"I," said the owl,
"With my spade and trowel
I'll dig his grave."

Who'll be the parson?
"I," said the rook,
"With my little book,
I'll be the parson."

Who'll be chief mourner?
"I," said the dove,
"I mourn for my love,
I'll be chief mourner."

Who'll sing a psalm?
"I," said the thrush,
"As I sit in a bush.
I'll sing a psalm."

Who'll carry the coffin?
"I," said the kite,
"If it's not in the night,
I'll carry the coffin."

Who'll toll the bell?
"I," said the bull,
"Because I can pull,
I'll toll the bell."

All the birds of the air
Fell sighing and sobbing,
When they heard the bell toll
For poor Cock Robin.

THE MOUSE AND THE CLOCK

Hickory, dickory, dock!
The mouse ran up the clock;
The clock struck one,
And down he run,
Hickory, dickory, dock!

THE BUNCH OF BLUE RIBBONS

THE BUNCH OF BLUE RIBBONS

Oh, dear, what can the matter be?
Oh, dear, what can the matter be?
Oh, dear, what can the matter be?
Johnny's so long at the fair

He promised he'd buy me a bunch of
blue ribbons,
He promised he'd buy me a bunch of
blue ribbons,
He promised he'd buy me a bunch of
blue ribbons,
To tie up my bonny brown hair.

HOT-CROSS BUNS

Hot-cross Buns!
Hot-cross Buns!
One a penny, two a penny,
Hot-cross Buns!

Hot-cross Buns!
Hot-cross Buns!
If ye have no daughters,
Give them to your sons.

BOBBY SHAFTOE

Bobby Shaftoe's gone to sea,
With silver buckles on his knee:
He'll come back and marry me,
Pretty Bobby Shaftoe!
Bobby Shaftoe's fat and fair,
Combing down his yellow hair;
He's my love for evermore,
Pretty Bobby Shaftoe.

THE WOMAN OF EXETER

There dwelt an old woman at Exeter;
When visitors came it sore vexed her,
So for fear they should eat,
She locked up all her meat,
This stingy old woman of Exeter.

SNEEZING

If you sneeze on Monday, you sneeze
    for danger;
Sneeze on a Tuesday, kiss a stranger;
Sneeze on a Wednesday, sneeze
    for a letter;
Sneeze on a Thursday, something
    better.
Sneeze on a Friday, sneeze for
    sorrow;
Sneeze on a Saturday,
    joy tomorrow.

PUSSY-CAT BY THE FIRE

Pussy-cat sits by the fire;
How can she be fair?
In walks the little dog;
Says: "Pussy, are you there?
How do you do, Mistress Pussy?
Mistress Pussy, how d'ye do?"
"I thank you kindly, little dog,
I fare as well as you!"

WHEN THE SNOW IS ON
THE GROUND

The little robin grieves
When the snow is on the ground,
For the trees have no leaves,
And no berries can be found.

The air is cold, the worms are hid;
For robin here what can be done?

Let's strow around some crumbs of
    bread,
And then he'll live till snow is gone.

THE YEAR

January brings the snow,
Makes our feet and fingers glow.

February brings the rain,
Thaws the frozen lake again.

March brings breezes loud and shrill,
Stirs the dancing daffodil.

April brings the primrose sweet,
Scatters daisies at our feet.

May brings flocks of pretty lambs,
Skipping by their fleecy dams.

June brings tulips, lilies, roses,
Fills the children's hands with posies.

Hot July brings cooling showers,
Apricots and gillyflowers.

August brings the sheaves of corn,
Then the harvest home is borne.

Warm September brings the fruit,
Sportsmen then begin to shoot.

Fresh October brings the pheasant,
Then to gather nuts is pleasant.

Dull November brings the blast,
Then the leaves are whirling fast.

Chill December brings the sleet,
Blazing fire and Christmas treat.

ROBIN-A-BOBBIN

Robin-a-Bobbin
Bent his bow,
Shot at a pigeon,
And killed a crow.

JOHN SMITH

Is John Smith within?
Yes, that he is.
Can he set a shoe?
Ay, marry, two.
Here a nail, there a nail,
Tick, tack, too.

RAIN

HANDY PANDY

Handy Pandy, Jack-a-dandy,
Loves plum cake and sugar candy.
He bought some at a grocer's shop,
And out he came, hop, hop, hop!

A NICK AND A NOCK

A nick and a nock,
A hen and a cock,
And a penny for my master.

THE SEASONS

Spring is showery, flowery, bowery;
Summer: hoppy, croppy, poppy;
Autumn: wheezy, sneezy, freezy,
Winter: slippy, drippy, nippy.

BILLY, BILLY

Billy, Billy, come and play
While the sun shines bright as day.

RAIN

Rain, rain, go away,
Come again another day;
Little Johnny wants to play.

JACK AND JILL

Jack and Jill went up the hill,
To fetch a pail of water;
Jack fell down, and broke his crown,
And Jill came tumbling after.

Then up Jack got and off did trot,
    As fast as he could caper,
To old Dame Dob, who patched his
    nob
With vinegar and brown paper.

The mischievous raven flew
    laughing away,
Bumpety, bumpety, bump!
And vowed he would serve them
    the same the next day,
Lumpety, lumpety lump!

CHRISTMAS

Christmas is coming, the geese are
    getting fat,
Please to put a penny in an old
    man's hat;
If you haven't got a penny a
    ha'penny will do,
If you haven't got a ha'penny, God
    bless you.

THE FARMER AND THE RAVEN

A farmer went trotting upon his gray
    mare,
Bumpety, bumpety, bump!
With his daughter behind him so
    rosy and fair,
Lumpety, lumpety, lump!

A raven cried croak! and they all
    tumbled down,
Bumpety, bumpety, bump!
The mare broke her knees, and the
    farmer his crown,
Lumpety, lumpety, lump!